Ryan's Pizza Party

SIMON SPOTLIGHT

An imprint of Simon & Schuster Children's Publishing Division · New York London Toronto Sydney New Delhi
1230 Avenue of the Americas, New York, New York 10020 · This Simon Spotlight edition September 2019
Text by May Nakamura · TM & © 2019 RTR Production, LLC, RFR Entertainment, Inc. and Remka, Inc., and Pocketwatch, Inc. Ryan ToysReview, Ryan's World and all related titles, logos and characters are trademarks of RTR Production, LLC, RFR Entertainment, Inc. and Remka, Inc. The pocket.watch logo and all related titles, logos and characters are trademarks of Pocketwatch, Inc. All Rights Reserved. Photos and illustrations of Ryan and Ryan's World characters copyright © RTR Production, LLC, RFR Entertainment, Inc. and Remka, Inc. Stock photos and illustrations copyright © istock.com · All rights reserved, including the right of reproduction in whole or in part in any form. SIMON SPOTLIGHT and colophon are registered trademarks of Simon & Schuster, Inc.
For more information about special discounts for bulk purchases, please contact Simon & Schuster Special Sales at 1-866-506-1949 or business@simonandschuster.com. · Manufactured in the United States of America 1119 LAK
2 4 6 8 10 9 7 5 3 · ISBN 978-1-5344-6144-4 · ISBN 978-1-5344-6145-1 (eBook)

This is not a cookbook. If you would like to make your own pizza, ask an adult to find you a recipe and to help you make it. Never use the kitchen without adult supervision.

Hi, I'm Ryan from Ryan ToysReview! Today I'm having a pizza party with all my friends. Yes, that means you're invited too!

I love pizza—it's my favorite food. What is your favorite kind of pizza? Do you like thick or thin crust? Tomato sauce or no tomato sauce?

My favorite is cheese pizza.

Sometimes I make pretend play pizza videos for my YouTube channel. One time I pretended to deliver pizza to my daddy and mommy. Another time I pretended to work at a pizza drive-through.

When I was really little, I even did the pizza challenge and made a pizza with chocolate candies, gummy bears, and other unusual toppings!

Look at all these toppings that we can use for our pizza party. There's...

pepperoni, sausage, peppers, onions, mushrooms, tomatoes,

broccoli, olives, and, of course, plenty of cheese.

Ding-dong!

That's the doorbell ringing. Combo Panda, Peck, Alpha Lexa, and Big Gil are here for the party... and they're all hungry!

Gus and Moe are going to be late, so we can start the party now. We'll just leave some leftover pizza for them.

For today's party we're going to make a pizza called Ryan's Super Special Pizza! It will be as big as the entire oven and have all the toppings that can fit. It's going to be a pizza full of pizzazz!

First, let's roll the dough into the shape of a pizza.

Then Combo Panda will spread the tomato sauce on the dough.

Next, Alpha Lexa will sprinkle the cheese all over—extra, extra cheese!

Now for the toppings: pepperoni, sausage, and all the veggies that we can fit. I have a feeling this pizza is going to taste *soooo* good.

Mommy helps me put the pizza in the oven. While it bakes, let's get ourselves something to drink. Do you want milk, water, or juice? You can also add ice if you want!

Mmmm. I can smell the pizza, and it's making my stomach grumble.

Do you think it's ready yet?

The cheese is bubbling, the crust is crisp, and the toppings look nice and fresh. Now all we need to do is cut the pizza, and then it will be ready to eat. One Ryan's Super Special Pizza, coming right out!

This might be the yummiest pizza I've ever eaten! I'm going to eat another slice before it all disappears.

Did you know that **350** pizza slices are eaten in America every second? That's more than one million slices an hour!

We were supposed to leave some pizza for Gus and Moe, but we ate it all up! It was so yummy that there's not even a crumb left. They're going to be at a pizza party without pizza. . . . What should we do?

Let's open up the box. The mystery pizza is . . .

yummy gummy pizza!

It looks like a pizza but tastes like a gummy: soft and sweet. How cool is that? It's the perfect dessert to end the pizza party!

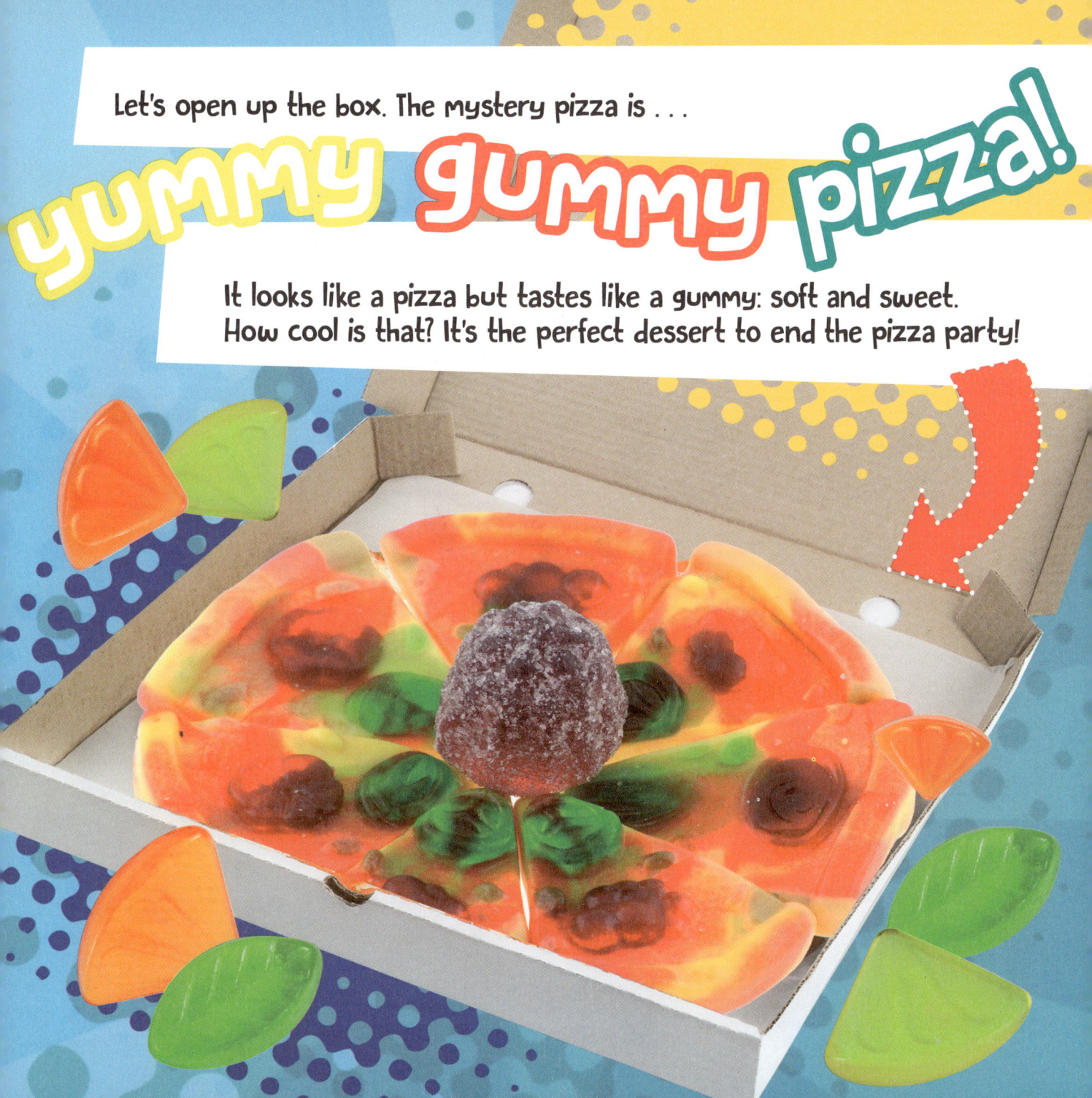

Thanks for coming to my pizza party. I hope you had a great time! I had a blast. Pizza always tastes better with friends.

I hope I see you again soon on my channel!